Titles in this series

Railway Series, No. 26

TRAMWAY ENGINES

by

THE REV. W. AWDRY

with illustrations by
GUNVOR AND PETER EDWARDS

EGMONT

First published in Great Britain 1972
This edition first published 2002
by Egmont Books Limited
239 Kensington High Street, London W8 6SA
This edition © Gullane (Thomas) LLC 2002

1 3 5 7 9 10 8 6 4 2

ISBN 1 4052 0356 0

Foreword

Thomas has been pestering me to write about his Branch Line. "After all," he said, "we are the importantest part of the whole railway."

"What can I write about?" I asked.

"Oh, lots of things—Percy's Woolly Bear, Toby's Tightrope and . . ."

". . . your Ghost," I added.

"Don't put that silly story in," said Thomas crossly.

I will, all the same. Thomas has been much too cocky lately. It will serve him right!

THE AUTHOR

Ghost Train

". . . And every year on the date of the accident it runs again, plunging into the gap, shrieking like a lost soul."

"Percy, what *are* you talking about?"

"The Ghost Train. Driver saw it last night."

"Where?" asked Thomas and Toby together.

"He didn't say, but it must have been on our line. He says ghost trains run as a warning to others. "Oooh!" he went on, "it makes my wheels wobble to think of it!"

"Pooh!" said Thomas. "You're just a silly little engine, Percy. I'm not scared."

"Thomas didn't believe in your ghost," said Percy, next morning.

His Driver laughed. "Neither do I. It was a 'pretend' ghost on television."

Percy was disappointed, but he was too busy all day with his stone trucks to think about ghosts. That evening he came back "light engine" from the harbour. He liked running at night. He coasted along without effort, the rails humming cheerfully under his wheels, and signal lights changing to green at his approach.

He always knew just where he was, even in the dark. "Crowe's Farm Crossing," he chuntered happily. "We shan't be long now."

Sam had forgotten that Mr Crowe wanted a load of lime taken to Forty-acre field. When he remembered, it was nearly dark. He drove in a hurry, bumped over the crossing, and sank his cart's front wheels in mud at the field gate.

The horse tried hard, but couldn't move it. The cart's tail still fouled the railway.

Sam gave it up. He unharnessed the horse, and rode back to the farm for help. "There's still time," he told himself. "The next train isn't due for an hour."

But he'd reckoned without Percy.

Percy broke the cart to smithereens, and lime flew everywhere. They found no one at the crossing, so went on to the nearest signalbox.

"Hullo!" said the signalman. "What have you done to Percy? He's white all over!"

Percy's Driver explained. "I'll see to it," said the signalman, "but you'd better clean Percy, or people will think he's a ghost!"

Percy chuckled. "Do let's pretend I'm a ghost, and scare Thomas. That'll teach him to say I'm a silly little engine!"

On their way they met Toby, who promised to help.

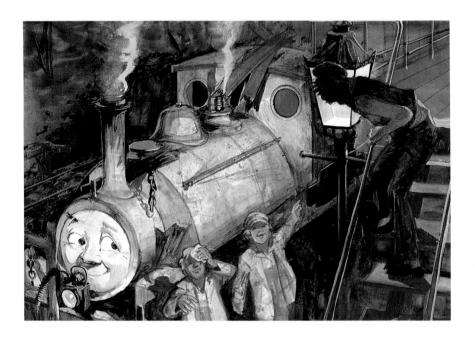

Thomas was being "oiled up" for his evening train, when Toby hurried in saying, "Percy's had an accident."

"Poor engine!" said Thomas. "Botheration! That means I'll be late."

"They've cleared the line for you," Toby went on, "but there's something worse—"

"Out with it, Toby," Thomas interrupted. "I can't wait all evening."

"—I've just seen something," said Toby in a shaky voice. "It *looked* like Percy's ghost. It s—said it w—was c—coming here t—to w—warn us."

"Pooh! Who cares? Don't be frightened, Toby. I'll take care of you."

Percy approached the shed quietly and glided through it. "Peeeeep! peeeeeeeeeeeep! pip! pip! pip! Peeeeeeeeeeeeeeeeeeeeep!" he shrieked.

As had been arranged, Toby's Driver and Fireman quickly shut the doors.

"Let me in! Let me in!" said Percy in a spooky voice.

"No, no!" answered Toby. "Not by the smoke of my chimney, chim chim!"

"I'll chuff and I'll puff, and I'll break your door in!"

"Oh dear!" exclaimed Thomas. "It's getting late. . . . I'd no idea. . . . I must find Annie and Clarabel. . . ."

He hurried out the other way.

Percy was none the worse for his adventure. He was soon cleaned; but Thomas never returned. Next morning Toby asked him where he'd been.

"Ah well," said Thomas. "I knew you'd be sad about Percy, and—er—I didn't like to—er—intrude. I slept in the Goods Shed, and . . . Oh!" he went on hurriedly, "sorry . . . can't stop . . . got to see a coach about a train," and he shot off like a jack rabbit.

Percy rolled up alongside. "Well! Well! Well!" he exclaimed. "What d'you know about that?"

"Anyone would think," chuckled Toby, "that our Thomas had just seen a ghost!"

Woolly Bear

GANGERS had been cutting the line-side grass, and "cocking" it.

The Fat Controller sells the hay to hill-farmers who want winter feed for their stock.

At this time of year, when Percy comes back from the harbour, he stops where they have been cutting. The men load up his empty wagons, and he pulls them to Ffarquhar. Toby then takes them to the hills. The farmers collect the hay from Toby's top station.

When in the wagons, the hay is covered to prevent it blowing about, but on the line-side it is stacked in the open air to dry.

"Wheeeeeeeeeesh!" Percy gave his ghostly whistle. "Don't be frightened, Thomas," he laughed, "it's only me!"

"Your ugly fizz is enough to frighten anyone," said Thomas crossly. "You're like—"

"Ugly indeed! I'm—"

"—a green caterpillar with red stripes," continued Thomas firmly. "You crawl like one too."

"I don't."

"Who's been late every afternoon this week?"

"It's the hay."

"I can't help that," said Thomas. "Time's time, and the Fat Controller relies on me to keep it. I can't if you crawl in the hay till all hours."

"Green caterpillar indeed!" fumed Percy. "Everyone says I'm handsome—or at least *nearly* everyone. Anyway, my curves are better than Thomas's corners."

He took his trucks to the harbour, and spent the morning shunting. "Thomas says I'm always late," he grumbled. "I'm never late—or at least only a few minutes. What's that to Thomas? He can always catch up time further on."

All the same, he and his Driver decided to start home early. It was most unfortunate that, just before they did, a crate of treacle was upset over him. They wiped the worst off, but he was still sticky when he puffed away.

The wind rose as they puffed along. Soon it was blowing a gale.

"Look at that!" exclaimed his Driver.

The wind caught the piled hay, tossing it up and over the track. The gangers tried to clear it, but more always came.

The line climbed here. "Take a run at it Percy," his Driver advised; so, whistling warningly, Percy gathered speed. But the hay made the rails slippery, and his wheels wouldn't grip. Time after time he stalled with spinning wheels and had to wait till the line ahead was cleared before he could start again.

The signalman climbed a telegraph pole, the Stationmaster paced the platform, passengers fussed, and Thomas seethed impatiently.

"Ten minutes late! I warned him. Passengers'll complain, and the Fat Controller. . . ."

The signalman shouted, the Stationmaster stood amazed, the passengers exclaimed and laughed as Percy approached.

"Sorry—I'm—late!" Percy panted.

"So I should hope," scolded Thomas; but he spoilt the effect as Percy drew alongside. "Look what's crawled out of the hay!" he chortled.

"What's wrong?" asked Percy.

"Talk about hairy caterpillars!" puffed Thomas as he started away. "It's worth being late to have seen you!"

When Percy got home his Driver showed him what he looked like in a mirror.

"Bust my buffers!" exclaimed Percy. "No wonder they all laughed. I'm just like a woolly bear! Please clean me before Toby comes."

But it was no good. Thomas told Toby all about it, and instead of talking about sensible things like playing ghosts, Thomas and Toby made jokes about "woolly bear" caterpillars and other creatures which crawl about in hay.

They laughed a lot, but Percy thought they were really being very silly indeed.

Mavis

MAVIS is a diesel engine belonging to the Ffarquhar Quarry Company. They bought her to shunt trucks in their sidings.

She is black, and has six wheels. These, like Toby's, are hidden by sideplates.

Mavis is young, and full of her own ideas. She is sure they are better than anybody else's.

She loves re-arranging things, and put Toby's trucks in different places every day. This made Toby cross.

"Trucks," he grumbled, "should be where you want them, when you want them."

"Fudge!" said Mavis, and flounced away.

At last Toby lost patience. "I can't waste time playing 'Hunt the Trucks' with you," he snapped. "Take 'em yourself."

Mavis was delighted. Taking trucks made her feel important.

At Ffarquhar she met Daisy. "Toby's an old fusspot," she complained.

Daisy liked Toby, but was glad of a diesel to talk to. "Steam engines," she said, "have their uses, but they don't understand. . . ."

"Toby says only steam engines can manage trucks properly. . . ."

"What rubbish!" put in Daisy, who knew nothing about trucks. "Depend upon it, my dear, anything steam engines do, we diesels can do better."

Toby's line crosses the main road behind Ffarquhar Station, and, for a short way, follows a farm lane. The rails here are buried in earth and ashes almost to their tops. In wet weather, animals, carts, and tractors make the lane muddy and slippery. Frost makes the mud rock-hard. It swells it too, preventing engine wheels from gripping the rails properly.

Toby found this place troublesome; so, when frost came, he warned Mavis and told her just what to do.

"I can manage, thank you," she said cheekily. "I'm not an old fusspot like you."

The trucks were tired of being pushed around by Mavis. "It's slippery," they whispered. "Let's push *her* around instead."

"On! On! On!" they yelled, as Mavis reached the "Stop" board; but Mavis had heard about Percy, and took no chances. She brought them carefully down to the lane, and stopped at the Level Crossing. There, her Second Man halted the traffic while the Guard unpinned the wagon brakes.

"One in the headlamp for fusspot Toby!" she chortled. She looked forward to having a good giggle about it with Daisy.

But she never got her giggle. She was so sure she was right, that she'd stopped in the wrong place.

In frosty weather Toby stops *before* reaching the lane, and while some of his trucks are still on the slope. This ensures that they can't hold him back, and their weight helps him forward till his wheels can grip again.

But Mavis had given the trucks the chance they wanted. "Hold back! Hold back!" they giggled.

"Grrrrrrr Up!" ordered Mavis. The trucks just laughed, and her wheels spun helplessly. She tried backing, but the same thing happened.

They sanded the rails, and tried to dig away the frozen mud, but only broke the spade.

Cars and lorries tooted impatiently.

"Grrrrr agh!" wailed Mavis in helpless fury.

"I warned her," fumed Toby. "I told her just where to stop. 'I can manage,' she said, and called me an old fusspot."

"She's young yet," soothed his Driver, "and. . . ."

"She can manage her trucks herself."

"They're *your* trucks really," his Driver pointed out. "Mavis isn't supposed to come down here. If the Fat Controller. . . ."

"You wouldn't tell, would you?"

"Of course not."

"Well then. . . ."

"But," his Driver went on, "if we don't help clear the line, he'll soon know all about it, and so shall we!"

"Hm! Yes!" said Toby thoughtfully.

An angry farmer was telling Mavis just what she could do with her train!

Toby buffered up. "Having trouble, Mavis? I *am* surprised!"

"Grrrrrroosh!" said Mavis.

With much puffing and wheel-slip, Toby pushed the trucks back. Mavis hardly helped at all.

The hard work made Toby's fire burn fiercely. He then reversed, stopping at intervals while his Fireman spread hot cinders to melt the frozen mud. "Goodbye," he called as he reached the crossing. "You'll manage now, I expect."

Mavis didn't answer. She took the trucks to the sheds, and scuttled home as quickly as she could.

Toby's Tightrope

THE Manager spoke to Mavis severely. "You are a very naughty engine. You have no business to go jauntering down Toby's line instead of doing your work up here."

"It's that Toby," protested Mavis. "He's a fusspot. He. . . ."

"Toby has forgotten more about trucks than you will ever know. You will put the trucks where he wants them and nowhere else."

"But. . . ."

"There are no 'buts'," said the Manager sternly. "You will do as you are told—or else. . . ."

Mavis stayed good for several days!

Mavis soon got tired of being good.

"Why shouldn't I go on Toby's line?" she grumbled. She started making plans.

At the Top Station, the siding arrangements were awkward. To put trucks where Toby wanted them Mavis had to go backwards and forwards taking a few at a time.

"If," she suggested to her Driver, "we used the teeniest bit of Toby's line, we could save all this bother."

Her Driver, unsuspicious, spoke to the Manager, who allowed them to go as far as the first Level Crossing.

Mavis chuckled; but she kept it to herself!

Frost hindered work in the Quarry, but a thaw made them busy again. More trucks than ever were needed. Some trains were so long that Mavis had to go beyond the Level Crossing.

This gave her ideas, and a chance to go further down the line without it seeming her fault.

"Can you keep a secret?" she asked the trucks.

"Yes! yes! yes!" they chattered.

"Will you bump me at the Level Crossing, and tell no one I asked you?"

The trucks were delighted, and promised.

It was unfortunate that Toby should have arrived while Mavis was elsewhere, and decided to shunt them himself.

They reached the Level Crossing, and Toby's brakes came on. This was the signal for the trucks.

"On! On! On!" they yelled, giving him a fearful bump. His Driver and Fireman, taken unawares, were knocked over in the cab, and before they could pick themselves up, Toby was away, with the trucks screaming and yelling behind him.

What none of them realised was that with the warmer weather melted snow from the mountains had turned a quiet stream into a raging torrent, and that the supports of the bridge they were approaching had already been undermined.

Toby and his crew saw it together. The bridge vanished before their eyes, leaving rails like tightropes stretched across the gap.

"Peep Peep Peeeeep!" whistled Toby.

His Driver, still dazed, fought for control. Shut regulator—reverser hard over—full steam against the trucks.

"Hold them, boy, hold them. It's up to you."

Nearer and nearer they came. Toby whistled despairingly.

Though their speed was reduced, braking was still risky, but it was all or nothing now. The Driver braked hard. Toby went into a squealing slide, groaned fearfully, and stopped, still on the rails, but with his wheels treading the tightrope over the abyss.

Mavis was horrified. She brought some men who anchored Toby with ropes while she pulled the trucks away. Then she ran to the rescue.

"Hold on, Toby!" she tooted. "I'm coming."

Ropes were fastened between the two engines. Toby still had steam and was able to help, so he was soon safe on firm track, and saying "Thank-you" to Mavis.

"I'm sorry about the trucks," said Mavis, "I can't think how you managed to stop them in time."

"Oh, well!" said Toby. "My Driver's told me about circus people who walk tightropes, but I just didn't fancy doing it myself!"

The Fat Controller thanked the Manager and his men for rescuing Toby from his "tightrope".

"A very smart piece of work," he said. "Mavis did well too, I hear."

Mavis looked ashamed. "It was my fault about those trucks, Sir," she faltered. "I didn't know. . . . But if I could. . . ."

"Could what?" smiled the Fat Controller.

"Come down the line sometimes, Sir. Toby says he'll show me how to go on."

"Certainly, if your Manager agrees."

And so it was arranged. Mavis is now a welcome visitor at Ffarquhar Shed. She is still young and still makes mistakes; but she is never too proud to ask Toby, and Toby always helps her to put things right.